My Favorite Dogs

CAVALIER KING CHARLES SPANIEL

Jinny Johnson

A⁺

Smart Apple Media

Published by Smart Apple Media,
an imprint of Black Rabbit Books
P.O. Box 3263, Mankato, Minnesota, 56002
www.blackrabbitbooks.com

Edited by Mary-Jane Wilkins
Designed by Hel James

Library of Congress Cataloging-in-Publication Data
Johnson, Jinny, author.
 Cavalier King Charles spaniel / Jinny Johnson.
     pages cm. -- (My favorite dogs)
 Summary: "Describes the characteristics of the Cavalier King Charles
Spaniel and how to care for it"-- Provided by publisher.
 Audience: K to grade 3.
 Includes index.
 ISBN 978-1-62588-176-2
 1. Cavalier King Charles spaniel--Juvenile literature. 2. Spaniels
--Juvenile literature. I. Title.
 SF429.C36D53 2015
 636.752'4--dc23
                    2014003941

Photo acknowledgements
t = top, b = bottom
title page Lee319/Shutterstock; page 3 Fuse/Thinkstock; 4 Lenkadan;
6 Michal Ninger; 7 Liliya Kulianionak; 8, 11 eleana, 12t WilleeCole,
b Eric Isselee; 13t, b Eric Isselee; 14 Chris Alcock; 15 vgm; 16 Waldemar
Dabrowski; 17 eleana/all Shutterstock; 18, 19 iStockphoto/Thinkstock;
20 WilleeCole; 21 Cameron Whitman; 22 Chris Alcock/all Shutterstock
Cover Eric Isselee/Shutterstock

Printed in China

DAD0053
032014
9 8 7 6 5 4 3 2 1

Contents

I'm a Cavalier King Charles Spaniel!

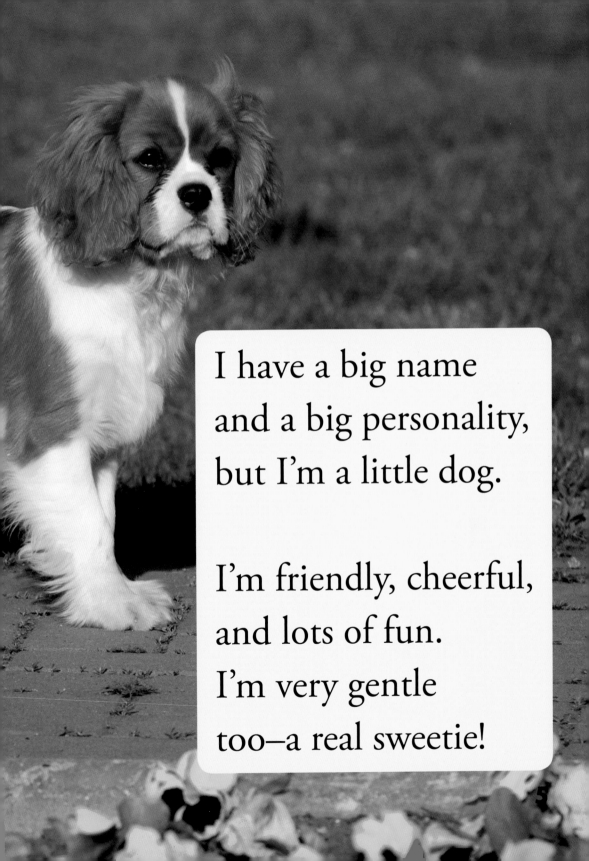

I have a big name
and a big personality,
but I'm a little dog.

I'm friendly, cheerful,
and lots of fun.
I'm very gentle
too—a real sweetie!

What I Need

I'm not difficult to look after but I don't like to be left alone. I love company and I'll follow you everywhere.

I like a walk every day and
I love to play games with you too.

I'm happy living in a house
or an apartment.

Don't leave me outdoors either.

The Cavalier King Charles

Color:
Chestnut and white
(Blenheim),
black, white and tan
(Tricolor),
ruby (solid red),
black and tan

Height at shoulder:
12-13 inches (30-33 cm)

Weight:
13-18 pounds (6-8 kg)

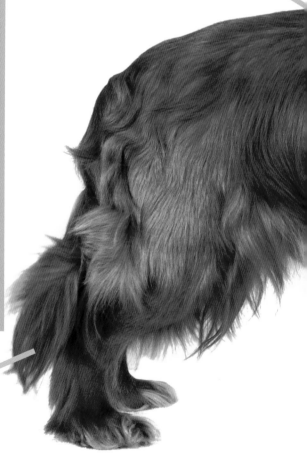

Straight back

Long, feathery tail

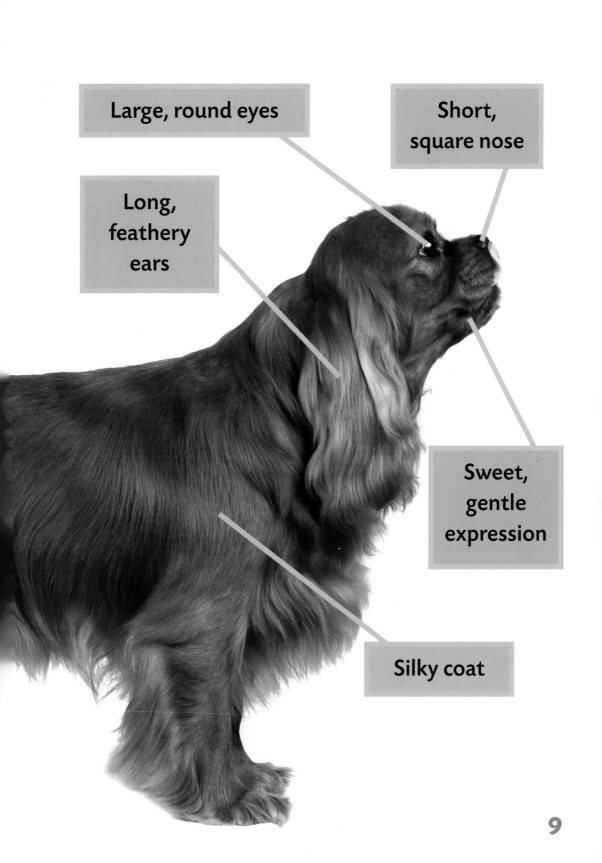

Large, round eyes

Short, square nose

Long, feathery ears

Sweet, gentle expression

Silky coat

9

All About Cavaliers

This little spaniel is named after Charles II, King of England from 1630-1685. You'll see these dogs in paintings of important people from this time.

Now Cavaliers are popular pets. They are good with children and like to be with other pets. They even get along well with cats.

Growing Up

Tiny pups need to be with their mom.

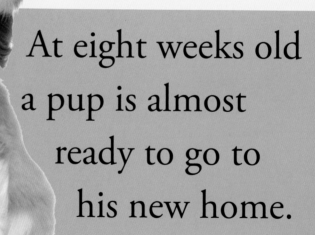

At eight weeks old a pup is almost ready to go to his new home.

A three-month-old puppy is full of energy and likes lots of care and attention.

Your little pup will grow up fast.

Be sure to buy your pup from a good, reliable breeder.

WHITING PUBLIC LIBRARY
1735 OLIVER STREET
WHITING, IN 46394
(219) 659-0269

13

Training Your Dog

Cavaliers love to please their owners, so they are not hard to train.

Be gentle and never punish
your dog while she is learning.

Cavaliers, like all dogs, love
to be praised and given a reward
when they do well.

Good Companion

Spaniels were once hunting dogs, but this particular type has been bred as a companion.

These dogs were once known as "comforter spaniels" and they like nothing more than sitting on a lap or cuddling up with you on the sofa.

At heart a Cavalier is still a hunting dog and will chase anything that moves. She may forget her training if she sees something exciting, so keep her close when you are out.

17

Therapy Dog

The Cavalier's loving nature makes her a good therapy dog. These dogs visit people in hospitals or places where petting a dog helps people feel better and more cheerful.

A Cavalier is not a good guard dog. She might bark, but will give everyone a friendly welcome.

Your Healthy Dog

This breed can have heart, eye and hip problems, so make sure your puppy is checked by a vet before buying. Take your pet to the vet regularly to make sure she stays well.

Brush your Cavalier's coat at least once a week and don't let those long ears get matted. Your dog will need bathing sometimes too, but make sure to comb out any tangles first.

Caring For Your Dog

You and your family must think carefully before buying a Cavalier King Charles Spaniel. She may live for 11 years.

Every day your dog must have food, water, and exercise,

as well as lots of love and care.
She will need to go to the vet for
regular checks and vaccinations.
When you go out or away on
vacation, you will have to make plans
for your dog to be looked after.

If you care
for your dog
properly, she
will be a happy,
healthy animal
and give you
lots of joy.

Useful Words

breed
A particular type of dog.

hunting dog
A dog that goes hunting with humans to track or bring back prey.

vaccinations
Injections given by the vet to protect your dog against certain illnesses.

Index